Subway Sonata

By Patricia Lakin Illustrated by Heather Maione

The Millbrook Press   Brookfield, Connecticut

For Lee because of your endless gifts of love and support.

And for the people who ride the subways of New York and see it as it truly is—

a place filled with music and vibrant individuals of all ages, races, and backgrounds.

— PL

In memory of my father, Sidney D. Ingram, the most creative man I know.   —HM

Published by The Millbrook Press, Inc.
2 Old New Milford Road
Brookfield, Connecticut 06804
www.millbrookpress.com

Copyright © 2001 by Patricia Lakin
Illustrations copyright © 2001 by Heather Harms Maione
All rights reserved

Book design by Tania Garcia
Printed in Hong Kong

Library of Congress Cataloging-in-Publication Data
Lakin, Pat.
    Subway sonata / by Patricia Lakin ; illustrated by Heather Harms Maione.
        p. cm.
    Summary: The New York City subway provides inspiration for a writer, a composer,
    a choreographer, and an artist, taking them in four different artistic directions.
    ISBN 0-7613-1464-4 (lib. bdg.)
    [1. Artists—Fiction. 2. Subways—Fiction. 3. New York (N.Y.)—Fiction.]
    I. Maione, Heather Harms, ill. II. Title.

PZ7. L1586 Sr 2001
[E]—dc21
                                                                00-029209

On a Monday morning, in a crowded subway car, people read, sleep, talk, or stare.

But four subway passengers — Carlos, Rachel, Paul, and Maria
— all strangers to each other — take everything in.

Most people leave the subway with no thoughts of this ride.
But these four passengers come out of the subway thinking about what they saw.

They carry their visions to work.

Carlos to the day-care center

Rachel in the cab she drives

Paul to the coffee shop

Maria to the bakery

When they come home and can be alone
with their thoughts, they can begin to work at their art.

Carlos, a writer, uses words
and the computer.

Rachel, a composer, uses
notes and a keyboard.

Paul, a choreographer, uses
his body and a mirror.

Maria, an artist, uses paints,
brushes, and a canvas.

At first their ideas are like lumps of clay that have to be chiseled away in order to find their form. They work for hours, days, and weeks. There are moments of frustration and doubt.

"A shy Russian boy on a subway...
maybe there is no story to write.
Or maybe it's me who can't write it."

"No! No! No! That's not the sound I want."

"I thought that step looked great yesterday. Today it looks STUPID!"

"Who am I kidding. I can't draw!"

But these four artists don't let go of their dream.
All four of them delve deep into their training to try to bring their visions to life.

"I have to write about a new immigrant boy who wants to believe in himself."

"There's music in the subway. I know it! I just have to keep believing in myself and try to find a way to get the rhythms across."

"That Spanish man had such grace and dignity. My dance must capture that spirit."

"That woman on the subway looked like one of Rembrandt's saints."

And when each least expects it, a magical moment occurs. Something clicks.

"That's it! The boy is learning from everything in the subway — the people, the signs, and . . . ."

"I need to write my piece in the classical style but . . . Hey! the noise of the city. What if I write it with nontraditional sounds and instruments!"

"I look like a Spanish dancer. That's it! I'll create a flamenco dance."

"Look at that sea of umbrellas with a big, white one in the middle. That's it! My lady is a saint with umbrella-like arms! I can't wait to get home to paint her."

Each artist goes back to work to polish and change. Some start all over again. But they all are happy to tackle their work for they know they're on the right track.

"I'm starting this book again. But I don't care. Now I know how the book has to be written."

"I'm tired. But I feel great! I was up half the night finishing my sonata. I'm so happy with the way it sounds. Want to hear the tape I made of it?"

"This flamenco music and my steps are perfect together."

"Oh, ya, baby! Twist and shout!"

One morning, in a crowded subway car, Carlos, Rachel, Maria, and Paul are not headed for work.
Carlos goes to his publisher to see the first copy of his book, *Pepito's Subway School*.

Rachel goes to a studio to rehearse with a singer and a steel drummer.
Her composition, *Sonata for the Seventh Avenue IRT,* will be performed in three weeks.

Paul goes to meet three other dancers and a classical guitarist for costume fittings.
His dance, *Flamenco Ballet,* will debut in two weeks.

Maria goes to a gallery that will show her work.
Her carefully wrapped painting is entitled *Savior of the Subway Car.*

With their projects done, each artist can take the time to enjoy other forms of art.
Carlos browses at an art gallery with his wife and friends.

"Look at this wonderful painting. This artist, Maria Ruiz, is very talented."

Rachel goes to the ballet with her friend.

"I love that flamenco dancer, Paul Nelson. And he's the choreographer, too."

Paul attends an outdoor concert with his mother and father.

"See, Pop. I'm not the only artist who finds the subways an inspiration."

Maria reads a new book to her daughter.

"Okay, okay, Anna. I'll read one more chapter!"

Four strangers . . . who created four works of art . . . all inspired on the same subway train.

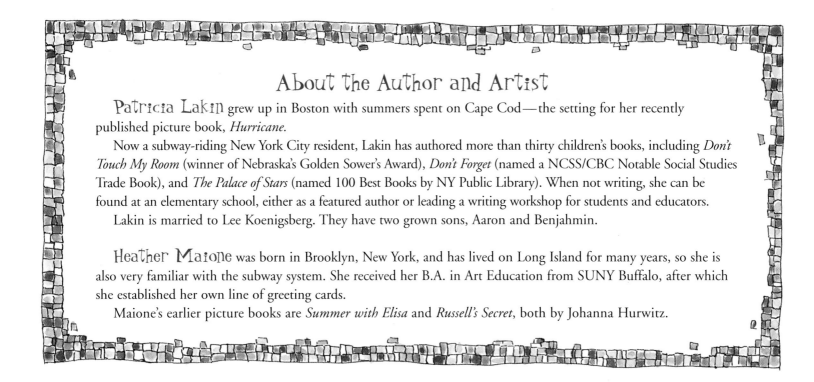

About the Author and Artist

Patricia Lakin grew up in Boston with summers spent on Cape Cod—the setting for her recently published picture book, *Hurricane*.

Now a subway-riding New York City resident, Lakin has authored more than thirty children's books, including *Don't Touch My Room* (winner of Nebraska's Golden Sower's Award), *Don't Forget* (named a NCSS/CBC Notable Social Studies Trade Book), and *The Palace of Stars* (named 100 Best Books by NY Public Library). When not writing, she can be found at an elementary school, either as a featured author or leading a writing workshop for students and educators.

Lakin is married to Lee Koenigsberg. They have two grown sons, Aaron and Benjahmin.

Heather Maione was born in Brooklyn, New York, and has lived on Long Island for many years, so she is also very familiar with the subway system. She received her B.A. in Art Education from SUNY Buffalo, after which she established her own line of greeting cards.

Maione's earlier picture books are *Summer with Elisa* and *Russell's Secret*, both by Johanna Hurwitz.